TO JAKE!

LET IT SNOW! ...PEOPLE

THE
BROTHERS

SNOWPEOPLE

RICK & RYAN ZEEB

SNOWPEOPLE

Illustrated by TRISH BURGIO

From Montague Island to McMurdo Sound,
in Lapland, in Greenland, and all the world 'round,

In places like these where the mercury drops
and icicles hang down from FROZEN ROOFTOPS...
These places have one thing in common, you know:

There's SURE to be snowpeople whenever there's snow.

I know you've all seen them, these PEOPLE of ice,
and probably made one at least once or twice.

With charcoal black eyes and CARROT STICK noses,
standing up straight in their stand-up-straight poses.
Their similar samenesses cover the ground,
the shape of their SHAPESES assuredly round.

Then one day a snowperson was heard to complain,
"WHY do we snowpeople all look the same?"

"It's true, we all DO look alike," said another.
"Dad looks like Mom looks like sister like brother.
And our CLOTHES ARE SO BORING, I hate to admit,
I'll be glad when it's spring just to lose the outfit."

"But look what we're made of," responded a third. "MILLIONS OF SNOWFLAKES, and everyone's heard there aren't TWO of those fellows exactly the same. They have different faces and facets and frames."

Some snowflakes are puny and some quite robust. With THAT the snowpeople decided they must try to be MORE like snowflakes.

"Let's try, if we dare,
and show we TOO have individual flair!"

"This year we'll be different. We'll trade in each nose,
we'll throw down our broomsticks, we'll wear fancy clothes."
And with this remark the snowpeople agreed,

"From monotonous wardrobes we all shall
be FREED!"

On wintry winds they had soon spread the word
so that all the snowpeople around the world heard...

"This winter, there's only ONE thing to do: ROLL YOURSELVES DOWN TO FIFTH AVENUE."

So on buses, in boxcars, in trolleys, on trains

from Dublin and Denver and Dayton they came . . .

Haberdashery hopping for
dungarees to drawers,

FRIGID FASHIONISTAS soon
filled up the stores.

They changed their APPEARANCE so by season's end,
once millions of snowpeople followed the trend,
You could tell Dad from Mom, and sister from brother,
when you compared one snowperson to another.

Each snowperson found their OWN PERSONAL STYLE, and they no longer need to eat charcoal to smile.

Now on Montague Island, in McMurdo Sound,
in all of the places SNOWPEOPLE abound,

It was finally discovered, no matter who's who,

DIFFERENT IS BRILLIANT.

It's what makes you

YOU!